This book belongs to . . .

_____

_____

For Jack Kitchin
and his Mum and Dad
N.McM.

First published in 2001 in Great Britain by Gullane Children's Books
This paperback edition first published 2002 by
Gullane Children's Books
185 Fleet Street, London EC4A 2HS
www.gullanebooks.com

3   5   7   9   10   8   6   4   2

Text and illustrations © Nigel McMullen 2001

The right of Nigel McMullen to be identified
as the author and illustrator of this work has been asserted by him
in accordance with the Copyright, Designs, and Patents Act, 1988.

ISBN 978-1-86233-636-0

Printed and bound in China

Not Me!

by Nigel McMullen

GULLANE™
CHILDREN'S BOOKS

Jack says Kenny is the
best brother in the world.

At breakfast, when
Jack knocked his plate on
the floor and Mum came
in looking cross...

Jack said,
"It **was** him!"

Kenny, who was too young to talk,
said nothing.

At lunchtime,
when Mum asked
who had eaten the
cake she'd taken
all morning
to make…

Jack said, "Not me!"
and hid the last slice in Kenny's nappy.

Kenny, who was too young to care, sat down.

Jack was building mudpies
when Mum called,
"You'd better stay clean!"

Jack said, "I **will**,"
and cleaned his hands on Kenny's shirt.

Kenny, who was too young to know what mud was, thought it tasted lovely.

At bathtime,
Jack was playing with
the squirty soap when
Mum asked who'd
made all the mess…

Jack said,
"It was him!"
and handed the bottle
to Kenny.

Kenny, who was too young to know better,
squirted Mum.

When they were warm and sleepy and ready for bed, Mum looked at Kenny and sighed, "You're so much trouble! But we wouldn't swap him, would we, Jack?"

Jack said, "Not me," and gave Kenny a kiss.

Kenny, who had never said anything before,
chose that moment to say

his very first word...

Other Gullane Children's Books for you to enjoy . . .

I Love You For Always and Forever
written by Jonathan Emmett
illustrated by Daniel Howarth

Longtail is faster and clever than Littletail.
But that won't be forever, says Longtail. Then he tells her
the one thing that will stay the same, always and forever. . .

Penguins
Liz Pichon

A little girl has dropped her camera into
the penguin enclosure. See how much fun the penguins
have had snapping when she finally gets it back!

Charles Fuge's Astonishing Animal ABC
Charles Fuge

Meet an arty aardvark, a dancing dodo,
a pirate penguin, an outraged owl . . . and find out which
curious creature is zig-zag-zooming its way to Z!

Imagine Me a Pirate!
Mark Marshall

Little Dog is as brave as brave can be. He's a pirate
on the open seas, an astronaut, a diver, an explorer. . .
But what does he like to do best of all?!